Level 4   Book 1

key

stories

Rapunzel

Stories adapted by Shirley Jackson
Illustrated by Shahrokh Na'el
Series designed by Jeannette Slater

Copyright © 2000 Egmont World Limited, a division of Egmont Holding Limited.
All rights reserved.
Published in Great Britain by Egmont World Limited, Deanway Technology Centre,
Wilmslow Road, Handforth, Cheshire SK9 3FB
Printed in Germany
ISBN 0 7498 4660 7
A CIP catalogue record for this book is available from the British Library

witch

long, golden hair

Rapunzel

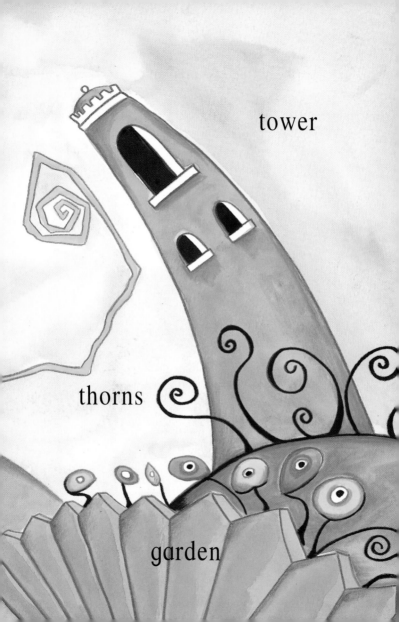

tower

thorns

garden

Once upon a time, a man and a woman lived next door to a witch.

The witch had a magic garden with magic herbs in it.

One day, the woman became ill.

"I must have some magic herbs," she said.

The man wanted to help his wife, but he was frightened of the witch.

The man climbed into the magic garden. He took some herbs. The witch saw him.

"I will give you the herbs, but you must give me your first baby," she shrieked.

The man was frightened, so he promised.

new words **took** **give**

Not long after this, the first baby came.

The witch shrieked, "Give me my baby!"

She took the baby to a high tower that had no doors.

new word   **doors**

The baby grew into a beautiful girl. The witch called her, "Rapunzel".

The witch liked to see Rapunzel every day.

"Rapunzel, Rapunzel, let down your golden hair," cried the witch.

new word   **Rapunzel's**

She climbed up Rapunzel's long, golden hair, and then they talked.

Every day, Rapunzel let down her long, golden hair.

And every day, the witch climbed up and they talked.

new word **every**

One day, a handsome prince
came to the tower.
He could hear beautiful
singing.
He waited to see who was
singing.

The prince saw Rapunzel.
He saw the witch climb up
Rapunzel's hair.

ew words **hear** **singing** **waited** **climb**

When the witch went away, the prince called, "Rapunzel, Rapunzel, let down your golden hair."

Rapunzel saw the prince. He was very handsome.

Rapunzel let down her long, golden hair.

The prince climbed up.

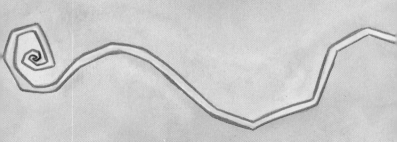

no new words

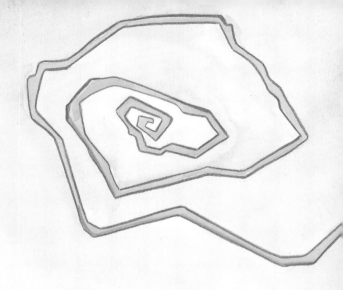

Rapunzel and the prince
became good friends.

They fell in love and
wanted to marry.

But Rapunzel could not
climb down the tower.

no new words

One day, the witch found out
about the prince.

She cut Rapunzel's hair
and made her go away.

Then the witch waited
for the prince.

new words **about cut**

When the prince came to the tower, he called for Rapunzel.

"Rapunzel, Rapunzel,
let down your golden hair,"
cried the prince.

The witch let down
Rapunzel's cut hair.

The prince climbed up.

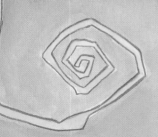

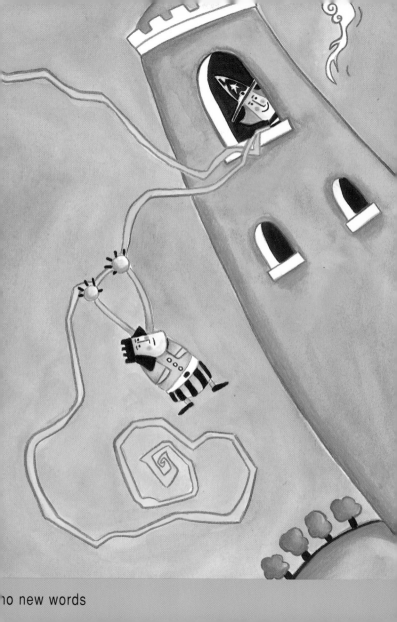

But the witch let go
of the cut hair.

The prince fell into some
thorns. The thorns cut the
prince and he could not see.

"I cannot live without
Rapunzel. I must find her!"
cried the prince.

new words **cannot without**

One day, the prince could hear beautiful singing.

It was Rapunzel!

Rapunzel was so happy that she cried. Her tears fell into the prince's cuts, and he could see again!

The prince and Rapunzel lived happily ever after.